P9-DJL-444

PRAISE FOR
THE GOLD CADILLAC

"A personal, poignant look at a black child's first experience
with institutional racism."   —*The New York Times*

"[The] first-person narrative allows readers to understand
the youthful perspective on the dehumanizing intentions of
racism. Clear language and logical, dramatic sequencing of
story events make this story bittersweet for adult readers but
important for the social development of beginning readers."
                                                —*School Library Journal*

AN AMERICAN BOOKSELLER "PICK OF THE LISTS"
AN NCSS-CBC NOTABLE CHILDREN'S TRADE BOOK
IN THE FIELD OF SOCIAL STUDIES

THE GOLD
CADILLAC

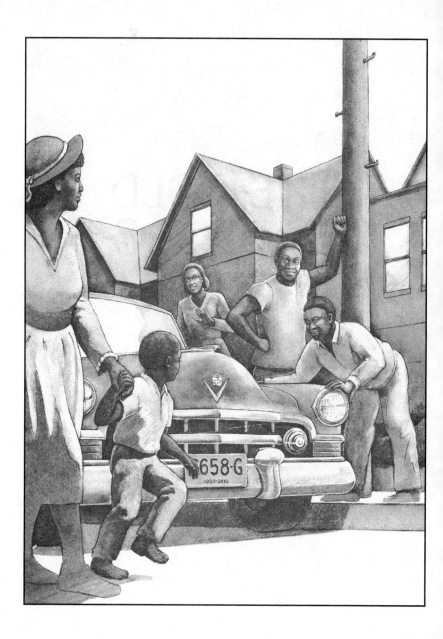

MILDRED D. TAYLOR

THE GOLD CADILLAC

PICTURES BY MICHAEL HAYS

PUFFIN BOOKS

PUFFIN BOOKS
An imprint of Penguin Random House LLC
375 Hudson Street
New York, New York 10014

First published in the United States of America
by Dial Books for Young Readers, 1987
First published by Puffin Books, 1998
This edition published by Puffin Books,
an imprint of Penguin Random House LLC, 2016

Text copyright © 1987 by Mildred D. Taylor
Illustrations copyright © 1987 by Michael Hays

Penguin supports copyright. Copyright fuels creativity, encourages
diverse voices, promotes free speech, and creates a vibrant culture. Thank
you for buying an authorized edition of this book and for complying with
copyright laws by not reproducing, scanning, or distributing any part of it in
any form without permission. You are supporting writers and allowing
Penguin to continue to publish books for every reader.

THE LIBRARY OF CONGRESS HAS CATALOGED THE DIAL BOOKS EDITION AS FOLLOWS:
Taylor, Mildred D. The gold Cadillac.
Summary: Two Black girls living in the North are proud of their
family's beautiful new Cadillac until they take it on a visit to the
South and encounter racial prejudice for the first time.
[1. Afro-Americans—Fiction. 2. Prejudices—Fiction.
3. Southern states—Race relations—Fiction. 4. Race relations—Fiction.]
I. Hays, Michael, ill. II. Title.
PZ7.T21723Go 1987 [Fic] 86-11526
ISBN: 0-8037-0342-2 (hardcover) ISBN: 0-8037-0343-0 (lib. bdg.)

Puffin Books ISBN 978-0-14-038963-0

Book design by Cara Petrus

Printed in the United States of America

39 40

To Mother-Dear,
who has always been there for all of us
with her love and strength and understanding

My sister and I were playing out on the front lawn when the gold Cadillac rolled up and my father stepped from behind the wheel. We ran to him, our eyes filled with wonder. "Daddy, whose Cadillac?" I asked.

And Wilma demanded, "Where's our Mercury?"

My father grinned. "Go get your mother and I'll tell you all about it."

"Is it ours?" I cried. "Daddy, is it ours?"

"Get your mother!" he laughed. "And tell her to hurry!"

Wilma and I ran off to obey as Mr. Pondexter next door came from his house to see what this new Cadillac was all about. We threw open the front door, ran through the downstairs front parlor and straight through the house to the kitchen where my mother was cooking and one of my aunts was helping her. "Come on, Mother-Dear!" we cried together. "Daddy say come on out and see this new car!"

"What?" said my mother, her face showing her surprise. "What're you talking about?"

"A Cadillac!" I cried.

"He said hurry up!" relayed Wilma.

And then we took off again, up the back stairs to the second floor of the duplex. Running down the hall, we banged on all the apartment doors. My uncles and their wives stepped to the doors. It was good it was a Saturday morning. Everybody was home.

"We got us a Cadillac! We got us a Cadillac!" Wilma and I proclaimed in unison. We had decided that the Cadillac had to be ours if our father was driving it and holding on to the keys. "Come on see!" Then we raced on, through the upstairs sunroom, down the front steps, through the downstairs sunroom, and out to the Cadillac. Mr. Pondexter was still there. Mr. LeRoy and Mr. Courtland from down the street were there too and all were admiring the Cadillac as my father stood proudly by, pointing out the various features.

"Brand-new 1950 Coupe deVille!" I heard one of the men saying.

"Just off the showroom floor!" my father said. "I just couldn't resist it."

My sister and I eased up to the car and peeked in. It was all gold inside. Gold leather seats. Gold carpeting. Gold dashboard. It was like no car we had owned before. It looked like a car for rich folks.

"Daddy, are we rich?" I asked. My father laughed.

"Daddy, it's ours, isn't it?" asked Wilma, who was older and more practical than I. She didn't intend to give her heart too quickly to something that wasn't hers.

"You like it?"

"Oh, Daddy, yes!"

He looked at me. "What 'bout you, 'lois?"

"Yes, sir!"

My father laughed again. "Then I expect I can't much disappoint my girls, can I? It's ours all right!"

Wilma and I hugged our father with our joy. My uncles came from the house and my aunts, carrying their babies, came out too. Everybody surrounded the car and owwed and ahhed. Nobody could believe it.

Then my mother came out.

Everybody stood back grinning as she approached the car. There was no smile on her face. We all waited for her to speak. She stared at the car, then looked at my father, standing there as proud as he could be. Finally she said, "You didn't buy this car, did you, Wilbert?"

"Gotta admit I did. Couldn't resist it."

"But . . . but what about our Mercury? It was perfectly good!"

"Don't you like the Cadillac, Dee?"

"That Mercury wasn't even a year old!"

My father nodded. "And I'm sure whoever buys it is going to get themselves a good car. But we've got ourselves a better one. Now stop frowning, honey, and let's take ourselves a ride in our brand-new Cadillac!"

My mother shook her head. "I've got food on the stove," she said and turning away walked back to the house.

There was an awkward silence and then my father said, "You know Dee never did much like surprises. Guess this here Cadillac was a bit too much for her. I best go smooth things out with her."

Everybody watched as he went after my mother. But when he came back, he was alone.

"Well, what she say?" asked one of my uncles.

My father shrugged and smiled. "Told me I bought this Cadillac alone, I could just ride in it alone."

Another uncle laughed. "Uh-oh! Guess she told you!"

"Oh, she'll come around," said one of my aunts. "Any woman would be proud to ride in this car."

"That's what I'm banking on," said my father as he went around to the street side of the car and opened the door. "All right! Who's for a ride?"

"We are!" Wilma and I cried.

All three of my uncles and one of my aunts, still holding her baby, and Mr. Pondexter climbed in with us and we took off for the first ride in the gold Cadillac. It was a glorious ride and we drove all through the city of Toledo. We rode past the church and past the school. We rode through Ottawa Hills where the rich folks lived and on into Walbridge Park and past the zoo, then along the Maumee River. But none of us had had enough of the car so my father put the car on the road and we drove all the way to Detroit. We had plenty of family there and everybody was just as pleased as could be about the Cadillac. My father told our Detroit relatives that he was in the doghouse with my mother about buying the Cadillac. My uncles told them she wouldn't ride in the car. All the Detroit family thought that was funny and everybody, including my father, laughed about it and said my mother would come around.

It was early evening by the time we got back home, and I could see from my mother's face she had not come around. She was angry now not only about the car, but that we had been gone so long. I didn't understand that, since my father had called her as soon as we reached Detroit to let her know where we were. I had heard him myself. I didn't understand either why she did not like that fine Cadillac and thought she was being terribly disagreeable with my father. That night as she tucked Wilma and me in bed I told her that too.

"Is this your business?" she asked.

"Well, I just think you ought to be nice to Daddy. I think you ought to ride in that car with him! It'd sure make him happy."

"I think you ought to go to sleep," she said and turned out the light.

Later I heard her arguing with my father. "We're suppose to be saving for a house!" she said.

"We've already got a house!" said my father.

"But you said you wanted a house in a better neighborhood. I thought that's what we both said!"

"I haven't changed my mind."

"Well, you have a mighty funny way of saving for it, then. Your brothers are saving for houses of their own and you don't see them out buying new cars every year!"

"We'll still get the house, Dee. That's a promise!"

"Not with new Cadillacs we won't!" said my mother and then she said a very loud good night and all was quiet.

The next day was Sunday and everybody figured that my mother would be sure to give in and ride in the Cadillac. After all, the family always went to church together on Sunday. But she didn't give in. What was worse she wouldn't let Wilma and me ride in the Cadillac either. She took us each by the hand, walked past the Cadillac where my father stood waiting and headed on toward the church, three blocks away. I was really mad at her now. I had been looking forward to driving up to the church in that gold Cadillac and having everybody see.

On most Sunday afternoons during the summertime, my mother, my father, Wilma, and I would go for a ride. Sometimes we just rode around the city and visited friends and family. Sometimes we made short trips over to Chicago or Peoria or Detroit to see relatives there or to Cleveland where we had relatives too, but we could also see the Cleveland Indians play. Sometimes we joined our aunts and uncles and drove in a caravan out to the park or to the beach. At the park or the beach Wilma and I would run and play. My mother and my aunts would spread a picnic and my father and my uncles would shine their cars.

But on this Sunday afternoon my mother refused to ride anywhere. She told Wilma and me that we could go. So we left her alone in the big, empty house, and the family cars, led by the gold Cadillac, headed for the park. For a while I played and had a good time, but then I stopped playing and went to sit with my father. Despite his laughter he seemed sad to me. I think he was missing my mother as much as I was.

That evening my father took my mother to dinner down at the corner café. They walked. Wilma and I stayed at the house chasing fireflies in the backyard. My aunts and uncles sat in the yard and on the porch, talking and laughing about the day and watching us. It was a soft summer's evening, the kind that came every day and was expected. The smell of charcoal and of barbecue drifting from up the block, the sound of laughter and music and talk drifting from yard to yard were all a part of it. Soon one of my uncles joined Wilma and me in our chase of fireflies and when my mother and father came home we were at it still. My mother and father watched us for awhile, while everybody else watched them to see if my father would take out

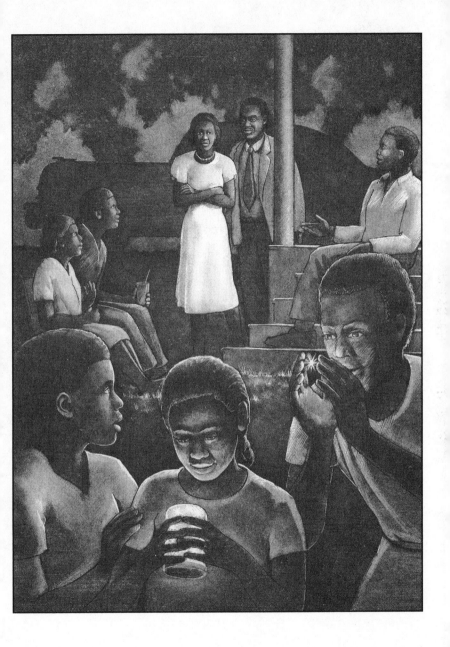

the Cadillac and if my mother would slide in beside him to take a ride. But it soon became evident that the dinner had not changed my mother's mind. She still refused to ride in the Cadillac. I just couldn't understand her objection to it.

Though my mother didn't like the Cadillac, everybody else in the neighborhood certainly did. That meant quite a few folks too, since we lived on a very busy block. On one corner was a grocery store, a cleaner's, and a gas station. Across the street was a beauty shop and a fish market, and down the street was a bar, another grocery store, the Dixie Theater, the café, and a drugstore. There were always people strolling to or from one of these places and because our house was right in the middle of the block just about everybody had to pass our house and the gold Cadillac. Sometimes people took in the Cadillac as they walked, their heads turning for a longer look as they passed. Then there were people who just outright stopped and took a good look before continuing on their way. I was proud to say that car belonged to my family. I felt mighty important as people called to me as I ran down the street. " 'Ey, 'lois! How's that Cadillac, girl? Riding fine?" I told my mother how much everybody liked that car. She was not impressed and made no comment.

Since just about everybody on the block knew everybody else, most folks knew that my mother wouldn't ride in the Cadillac. Because of that, my father took a lot of good-natured kidding from the men. My mother got kidded too as the women said if she didn't ride in that car, maybe some other woman would. And everybody laughed about it and began to bet on who would give in first, my mother or my father. But then my father said he was going to drive the car south into Mississippi to visit my grandparents and everybody stopped laughing.

My uncles stopped.

So did my aunts.

Everybody.

"Look here, Wilbert," said one of my uncles, "it's too dangerous. It's like putting a loaded gun to your head."

"I paid good money for that car," said my father. "That gives me a right to drive it where I please. Even down to Mississippi."

My uncles argued with him and tried to talk him out of driving the car south. So did my aunts and so did the neighbors, Mr. LeRoy, Mr. Courtland, and Mr. Pondexter. They said it was a dangerous thing, a mighty dangerous thing, for a black man to drive an expensive car into the rural South.

"Not much those folks hate more'n to see a northern Negro coming down there in a fine car," said Mr. Pondexter. "They see those Ohio license plates, they'll figure you coming down uppity, trying to lord your fine car over them!"

I listened, but I didn't understand. I didn't understand why they didn't want my father to drive that car south. It was his.

"Listen to Pondexter, Wilbert!" cried another uncle. "We might've fought a war to free people overseas, but we're not free here! Man, those white folks down south'll lynch you soon's look at you. You know that!"

Wilma and I looked at each other. Neither one of us knew what *lynch* meant, but the word sent a shiver through us. We held each other's hand.

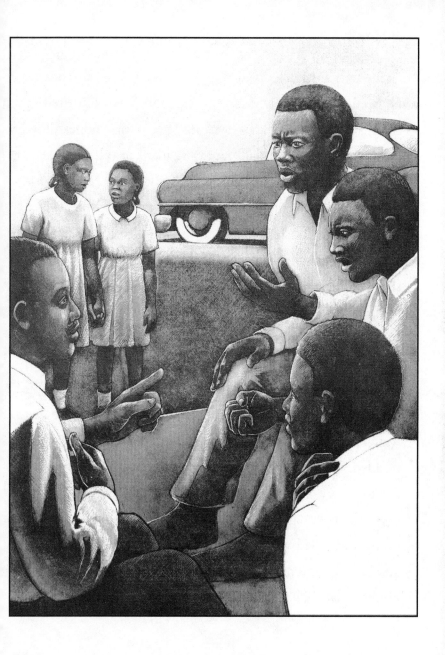

My father was silent, then he said: "All my life I've had to be heedful of what white folks thought. Well, I'm tired of that. I worked hard for everything I got. Got it honest, too. Now I got that Cadillac because I liked it and because it meant something to me that somebody like me from Mississippi could go and buy it. It's my car, I paid for it, and I'm driving it south."

My mother, who had said nothing through all this, now stood. "Then the girls and I'll be going too," she said.

"No!" said my father.

My mother only looked at him and went off to the kitchen.

My father shook his head. It seemed he didn't want us to go. My uncles looked at each other, then at my father. "You set on doing this, we'll all go," they said. "That way we can watch out for each other." My father took a moment and nodded. Then my aunts got up and went off to their kitchens too.

All the next day my aunts and my mother cooked and the house was filled with delicious smells. They fried chicken and baked hams and cakes and sweet potato pies and mixed potato salad. They filled jugs with water and punch and coffee. Then they packed everything in huge picnic baskets along with bread and boiled eggs, oranges and apples, plates and napkins, spoons and forks and cups. They placed all that food on the back seats of the cars. It was like a grand, grand picnic we were going on, and Wilma and I were mighty excited. We could hardly wait to start.

My father, my mother, Wilma, and I got into the Cadillac. My uncles, my aunts, my cousins got into the Ford, the Buick, and the Chevrolet, and we rolled off in our caravan headed south. Though my mother was finally riding in the Cadillac, she had no praise for it. In fact, she said nothing about it at all. She still seemed upset and since she still seemed to feel the same about the car, I wondered why she had insisted upon making this trip with my father.

We left the city of Toledo behind, drove through Bowling Green and down through the Ohio countryside of farms and small towns, through Dayton and Cincinnati, and across the Ohio River into Kentucky. On the other side of the river my father stopped the car and looked back at Wilma and me and said, "Now from here on, whenever we stop and there're white people around, I don't want either one

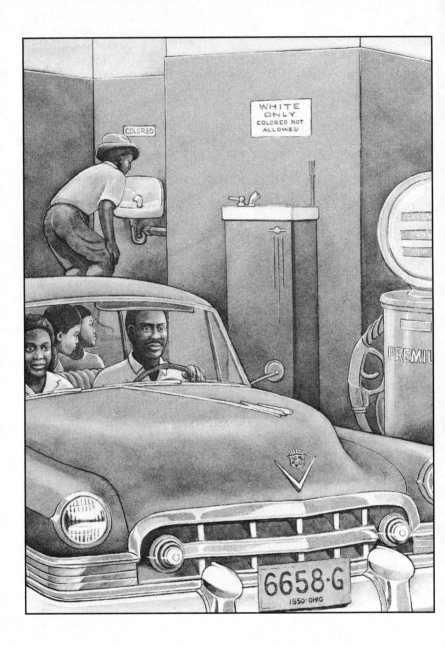

of you to say a word. *Not one word!* Your mother and I'll do all the talking. That understood?"

"Yes, sir," Wilma and I both said, though we didn't truly understand why.

My father nodded, looked at my mother and started the car again. We rolled on, down Highway 25 and through the bluegrass hills of Kentucky. Soon we began to see signs. Signs that read: WHITE ONLY, COLORED NOT ALLOWED. Hours later, we left the Bluegrass State and crossed into Tennessee. Now we saw even more of the signs saying: WHITE ONLY, COLORED NOT ALLOWED. We saw the signs above water fountains and in restaurant windows. We saw them in ice cream parlors and at hamburger stands. We saw them in front of hotels and motels, and on the restroom doors of filling stations. I didn't like the signs. I felt as if I were in a foreign land.

I couldn't understand why the signs were there and I asked my father what the signs meant. He said they meant we couldn't drink from the water fountains. He said they meant we couldn't stop to sleep in the motels. He said they meant we couldn't stop to eat in the restaurants. I looked at the grand picnic basket I had been enjoying so much. Now I understood why my mother had packed it. Suddenly the picnic did not seem so grand.

Finally we reached Memphis. We got there at a bad time. Traffic was heavy and we got separated from the rest of the family. We tried to find them but it was no use. We had to go on alone. We reached the Mississippi state line and soon after we heard a police siren. A police car came up behind us. My father slowed the Cadillac, then stopped. Two white policemen got out of their car. They eyeballed the Cadillac and told my father to get out.

"Whose car is this, boy?" they asked.

I saw anger in my father's eyes. "It's mine," he said.

"You're a liar," said one of the policemen. "You stole this car."

"Turn around, put your hands on top of that car and spread eagle," said the other policeman.

My father did as he was told. They searched him and I didn't understand why. I didn't understand either why they had called my father a liar and didn't believe that the Cadillac was his. I wanted to ask but I remembered my father's

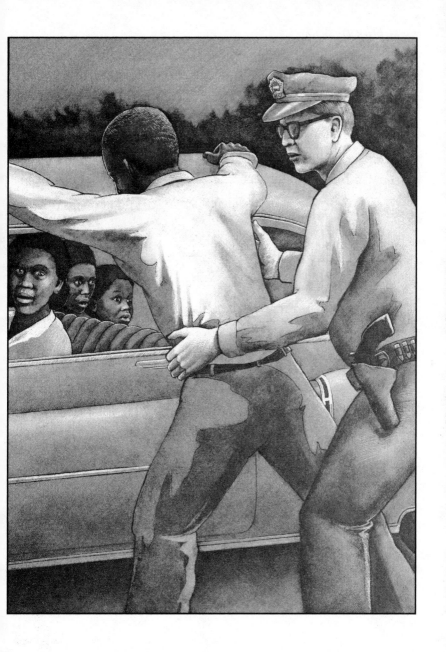

warning not to say a word and I obeyed that warning.

The policemen told my father to get in the back of the police car. My father did. One policeman got back into the police car. The other policeman slid behind the wheel of our Cadillac. The police car started off. The Cadillac followed. Wilma and I looked at each other and at our mother. We didn't know what to think. We were scared.

The Cadillac followed the police car into a small town and stopped in front of the police station. The policeman stepped out of our Cadillac and took the keys. The other policeman took my father into the police station.

"Mother-Dear!" Wilma and I cried. "What're they going to do to our daddy? They going to hurt him?"

"He'll be all right," said my mother. "He'll be all right." But she didn't sound so sure of that. She seemed worried.

We waited. More than three hours we waited. Finally my father came out of the police station. We had lots of questions to ask him. He said the police had given him a ticket for speeding and locked him up. But then the judge had come. My father had paid the ticket and they had let him go.

He started the Cadillac and drove slowly out of the town, below the speed limit. The police car followed us. People standing on steps and sitting on porches and in front of stores stared at us as we passed. Finally we were out of the town. The police car still followed. Dusk was falling. The night grew black and finally the police car turned around and left us.

We drove and drove. But my father was tired now and my grandparents' farm was still far away. My father said he had to get some sleep and since my mother didn't drive, he pulled into a grove of trees at the side of the road and stopped.

"I'll keep watch," said my mother.

"Wake me if you see anybody," said my father.

"Just rest," said my mother.

So my father slept. But that bothered me. I needed him awake. I was afraid of the dark and of the woods and of whatever lurked there. My father was the one who kept us safe, he and my uncles. But already the police had taken my father away from us once today and my uncles were lost.

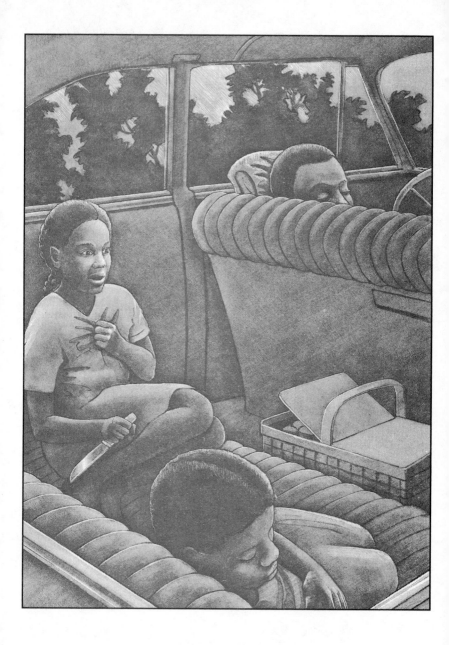

"Go to sleep, baby," said my mother. "Go to sleep."

But I was afraid to sleep until my father woke. I had to help my mother keep watch. I figured I had to help protect us too, in case the police came back and tried to take my father away again. There was a long, sharp knife in the picnic basket and I took hold of it, clutching it tightly in my hand. Ready to strike, I sat there in the back of the car, eyes wide, searching the blackness outside the Cadillac. Wilma, for a while, searched the night too, then she fell asleep. I didn't want to sleep, but soon I found I couldn't help myself as an unwelcome drowsiness came over me. I had an uneasy sleep and when I woke it was dawn and my father was gently shaking me. I woke with a start and my hand went up, but the knife wasn't there. My mother had it.

My father took my hand. "Why were you holding the knife, 'lois?" he asked.

I looked at him and at my mother. "I—I was scared," I said.

My father was thoughtful. "No need to be scared now, sugar," he said. "Daddy's here and so is Mother-Dear."

Then after a glance at my mother, he got out of the car, walked to the road, looked down it one way, then the other. When he came back and started the motor, he turned the Cadillac north, not south.

"What're you doing?" asked my mother.

"Heading back to Memphis," said my father. "Cousin Halton's there. We'll leave the Cadillac and get his car. Driving this car any farther south with you and the girls in the car, it's just not worth the risk."

And so that's what we did. Instead of driving through Mississippi in golden splendor, we traveled its streets and roads and highways in Cousin Halton's solid, yet not so splendid, four-year-old Chevy. When we reached my grandparents' farm, my uncles and aunts were already there. Everybody was glad to see us. They had been worried. They asked about the Cadillac. My father told them what had happened, and they nodded and said he had done the best thing.

We stayed one week in Mississippi. During that week I often saw my father, looking deep in thought, walk off alone across the family land. I saw my mother watching him. One day I ran after my father, took his hand, and walked the land with him. I asked him all the questions that were on my mind. I asked him why the policemen had treated him the way they had and why people didn't want us to eat in the restaurants or drink from the water fountains or sleep in the hotels. I told him I just didn't understand all that.

My father looked at me and said that it all was a difficult thing to understand and he didn't really understand it himself. He said it all had to do with the fact that black people had once been forced to be slaves. He said it had to do with our skins being colored. He said it had to do with stupidity and ignorance. He said it had to do with the law, the law that said we could be treated like this here in the South. And for that matter, he added, any other place in these United States where folks thought the same as so many folks did here in the South. But he also said, "I'm hoping one day though we can drive that long road down here and there won't be any signs. I'm hoping one day the police won't stop us just because of the color of our skins and we're riding in a gold Cadillac with northern plates."

When the week ended, we said a sad good-bye to my grandparents and all the Mississippi family and headed in a caravan back toward Memphis. In Memphis we returned Cousin Halton's car and got our Cadillac. Once we were home my father put the Cadillac in the garage and didn't drive it. I didn't hear my mother say any more about the Cadillac. I didn't hear my father speak of it either.

Some days passed and then on a bright Saturday afternoon while Wilma and I were playing in the backyard, I saw my father go into the garage. He opened the garage doors wide so the sunshine streamed in, and began to shine the Cadillac. I saw my mother at the kitchen window staring out across the yard at my father. For a long time, she stood there watching my father shine his car. Then she came out and crossed the yard to the garage and I heard her say, "Wilbert, you keep the car."

He looked at her as if he had not heard.

"You keep it," she repeated and turned and walked back to the house.

My father watched her until the back door had shut behind her. Then he went on shining the car and soon began to sing. About an hour later he got into the car and drove away. That evening when he came back he was walking. The Cadillac was nowhere in sight.

"Daddy, where's our new Cadillac?" I demanded to know. So did Wilma.

He smiled and put his hand on my head. "Sold it," he said as my mother came into the room.

"But how come?" I asked. "We poor now?"

"No, sugar. We've got more money towards our new house now and we're all together. I figure that makes us about the richest folks in the world." He smiled at my mother and she smiled too and came into his arms.

After that we drove around in an old 1930s Model A Ford my father had. He said he'd factory-ordered us another Mercury, this time with my mother's approval. Despite that, most folks on the block figured we had fallen on hard times after such a splashy showing of good times and some folks even laughed at us as the Ford rattled around the city. I must admit that at first I was pretty much embarrassed to be riding around in that old Ford after the splendor of the Cadillac. But my father said to hold my head high.

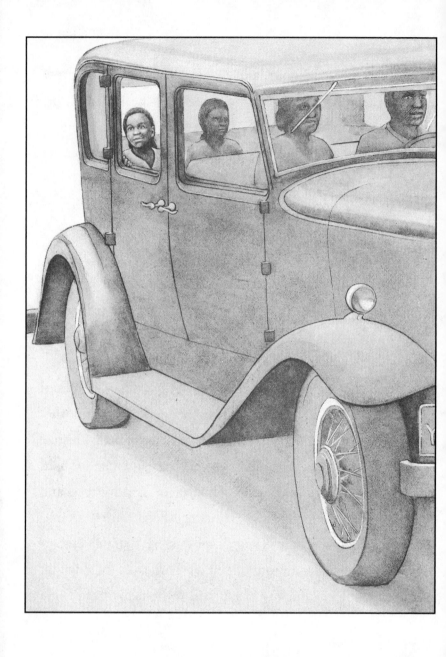

We and the family knew the truth. As fine as the Cadillac had been, he said, it had pulled us apart for awhile. Now, as ragged and noisy as that old Ford was, we all rode in it together and we were a family again. So I held my head high.

Still though, I thought often of that Cadillac. We had had the Cadillac only a little more than a month, but I wouldn't soon forget its splendor or how I'd felt riding around inside it. I wouldn't soon forget either the ride we had taken south in it. I wouldn't soon forget the signs, the policemen, or my fear. I would remember that ride and the gold Cadillac all my life.

Author's Note

For a few years when I was a child, I lived in a big house on a busy street with my mother, my father, my sister, and many aunts and uncles and cousins. We were originally a Mississippi family who had migrated to the industrial North during and after World War II. My father was the first of the family to go to the North and that was when I was only three weeks old. When I was three months old, my mother, my older sister, and I followed. A year after our arrival, my parents bought the big house on the busy street. During the next nine years, aunts and uncles and cousins from both sides of the family arrived yearly from Mississippi and stayed in that big house with us until they had earned enough to rent another place or buy houses on their own.

I loved those years.

There were always cousins to play with. There was always an aunt or uncle to talk to when my parents were busy, and there seemed always to be fun things to do and plenty of people to do them with. On the weekends the whole houseful of family often did things together. Because my father, my uncles, and my older male cousins all loved cars, we often rode in a caravan out to the park where the men would park their cars in a long, impressive row and shine them in the shade of the trees while the women spread a picnic and chatted, and my sister, younger cousins, and I ran and played. Sometimes we traveled to nearby cities to see other family members or to watch a baseball game. And sometimes we took even longer trips, down country highways into that land called the South.

I have many good memories of those years, including the year my father brought home a brand-new Cadillac. I also have memories of those years that long troubled me. I have woven some of those memories into this story of fiction called *The Gold Cadillac*.

TURN THE PAGE FOR AN EXCERPT FROM
MILDRED D. TAYLOR's
NEWBERY AWARD—WINNING NOVEL—

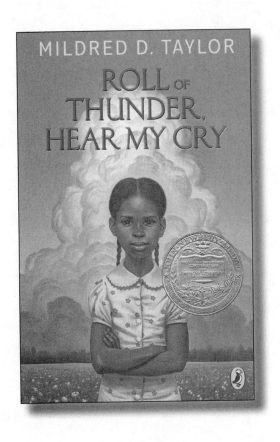

Text copyright © 1976 by Mildred D. Taylor

1

"Little Man, would you come on? You keep it up and you're gonna make us late."

My youngest brother paid no attention to me. Grasping more firmly his newspaper-wrapped notebook and his tin-can lunch of cornbread and oil sausages, he continued to concentrate on the dusty road. He lagged several feet behind my other brothers, Stacey and Christopher-John, and me, attempting to keep the rusty Mississippi dust from swelling with each step and drifting back upon his shiny black shoes and the cuffs of his corduroy pants by lifting each foot high before setting it gently down again. Always meticulously neat, six-year-old Little Man never allowed dirt or tears or stains to mar anything he owned. Today was no exception.

"You keep it up and make us late for school, Mama's gonna wear you out," I threatened, pulling with exasperation at the high collar of the Sunday dress Mama had made me wear for the first day of school—as if that event were something special. It seemed to me that showing up at school at all on a bright August-like October morning made for running the cool forest trails and wading barefoot in the forest pond was concession enough; Sunday clothing was asking too much. Christopher-John and Stacey were not too pleased about the clothing or school either. Only Little Man, just beginning his school career, found the prospects of both intriguing.

"Y'all go ahead and get dirty if y'all wanna," he replied without even looking up from his studied steps. "Me, I'm gonna stay clean."

"I betcha Mama's gonna 'clean' you, you keep it up," I grumbled.

"Ah, Cassie, leave him be," Stacey admonished, frowning and kicking testily at the road.

"I ain't said nothing but—"

Stacey cut me a wicked look and I grew silent. His disposition had been irritatingly sour lately. If I hadn't known the cause of it, I could have forgotten very easily that he was, at twelve, bigger than I, and that I had promised Mama to arrive at school looking clean and ladylike. "Shoot," I mumbled finally, unable to restrain myself from further comment, "it ain't my fault you gotta be in Mama's class this year."

Stacey's frown deepened and he jammed his fists into his pockets, but said nothing.

Christopher-John, walking between Stacey and me, glanced uneasily at both of us but did not interfere. A short, round boy of seven, he took little interest in troublesome things, preferring to remain on good terms with everyone. Yet he was always sensitive to others and now, shifting the handle of his lunch can from his right hand to his right wrist and his smudged notebook from his left hand to his left armpit, he stuffed his free hands into his pockets and attempted to make his face as moody as Stacey's and as cranky as mine. But after a few moments he seemed to forget that he was supposed to be grouchy and began whistling cheerfully. There was little that could make Christopher-John unhappy for very long, not even the thought of school.

I tugged again at my collar and dragged my feet in the dust, allowing it to sift back onto my socks and shoes like gritty red snow. I hated the dress. And the shoes. There was little I could do in a dress, and as for shoes, they imprisoned freedom-loving feet accustomed to the feel of the warm earth.

"Cassie, stop that," Stacey snapped as the dust billowed in swirling clouds around my feet. I looked up sharply, ready to protest. Christopher-John's whistling increased to a raucous, nervous shrill, and grudgingly I let the matter drop and trudged along in moody silence, my brothers growing as pensively quiet as I.

Before us the narrow, sun-splotched road wound like a lazy red serpent dividing the high forest bank of quiet, old trees on the left from the cotton field, forested by giant green and purple stalks, on the right. A barbed-wire fence ran the length of the deep field, stretching eastward for over a quarter of a mile until it met the sloping green pasture that signaled the end of our family's four hundred acres. An ancient oak tree on the slope, visible even now, was the official dividing mark between Logan land and the beginning of a dense forest. Beyond the protective fencing of the forest, vast farming fields, worked by a multitude of share-cropping families, covered two thirds of a ten-square-mile plantation. That was Harlan Granger land.

Once our land had been Granger land too, but the Grangers had sold it during Reconstruction to a Yankee for tax money. In 1887, when the land was up for sell again, Grandpa had bought two hundred acres of it, and in 1918, after the first two hundred acres had been paid off, he had bought another two hundred. It was good rich land, much of it still virgin forest, and there was no debt on half of it. But there was a mortgage on the two hundred acres bought in 1918 and there were taxes on the full four hundred, and for the past three years there had not been enough money from the cotton to pay both and live on too.

That was why Papa had gone to work on the railroad.

In 1930 the price of cotton dropped. And so, in the spring of 1931, Papa set out looking for work, going as far north as Memphis and as far south as the Delta country. He had gone west too, into Louisiana. It was there he found work laying track for the railroad. He worked the remainder of the year away from us, not returning until the deep winter when the ground was cold and barren. The following spring after the planting was finished, he did the same. Now it was 1933, and Papa was again in Louisiana laying track.

I asked him once why he had to go away, why the land was so important. He took my hand and said in his quiet way: "Look out there, Cassie girl. All that belongs to you. You ain't never had to live on nobody's place but your own and long as I live and the family survives, you'll never have to. That's important. You may not understand that now, but one day you will. Then you'll see."

I looked at Papa strangely when he said that, for I knew that all the land did not belong to me. Some of it belonged to Stacey, Christopher-John, and Little Man, not to mention the part that belonged to Big Ma, Mama, and Uncle Hammer, Papa's older brother who lived in Chicago. But Papa never divided the land in his mind; it was simply Logan land. For it he would work the long, hot summer pounding steel; Mama would teach and run the farm; Big Ma, in her sixties, would work like a woman of twenty in the fields and keep the house; and the boys and I would wear threadbare clothing washed to dishwater color; but always, the taxes and the mortgage would be paid. Papa said that one day I would understand.

I wondered.

When the fields ended and the Granger forest fanned both sides of the road with long overhanging branches, a tall, emaciated-looking boy popped suddenly from a forest trail and swung a thin arm around Stacey. It was T.J. Avery. His younger brother Claude emerged a moment later, smiling weakly as if it pained him to do so. Neither boy had on shoes, and their Sunday clothing, patched and worn, hung loosely upon their frail frames. The Avery family share-cropped on Granger land.

"Well," said T.J., jauntily swinging into step with Stacey, "here we go again startin' another school year."

"Yeah," sighed Stacey.

"Ah, man, don't look so down," T.J. said cheerfully. "Your mama's really one great teacher. I should know." He certainly should. He had failed Mama's class last year and was now returning for a second try.

"Shoot! You can say that," exclaimed Stacey. "You don't have to spend all day in a classroom with your mama."

"Look on the bright side," said T.J. "Jus' think of the advantage you've got. You'll be learnin' all sorts of stuff 'fore the rest of us. . . ." He smiled slyly. "Like what's on all them tests."

Stacey thrust T.J.'s arm from his shoulders. "If that's what you think, you don't know Mama."

"Ain't no need gettin' mad," T.J. replied undaunted.

"Jus' an idea." He was quiet for a moment, then announced, "I betcha I could give y'all an earful 'bout that burnin' last night."

"Burning? What burning?" asked Stacey.

"Man, don't y'all know nothin'? The Berrys' burnin'. I thought y'all's grandmother went over there last night to see 'bout 'em."

Of course we knew that Big Ma had gone to a sick house last night. She was good at medicines and people often called her instead of a doctor when they were sick. But we didn't know anything about any burnings, and I certainly didn't know anything about any Berrys either.

"What Berrys he talking 'bout, Stacey?" I asked. "I don't know no Berrys."

"They live way over on the other side of Smellings Creek. They come up to church sometimes," said Stacey absently. Then he turned back to T.J. "Mr. Lanier come by real late and got Big Ma. Said Mr. Berry was low sick and needed her to help nurse him, but he ain't said nothing 'bout no burning."

"He's low sick all right—'cause he got burnt near to death. Him and his two nephews. And you know who done it?"

"Who?" Stacey and I asked together.

"Well, since y'all don't seem to know nothin'," said T.J., in his usual sickening way of nursing a tidbit of information to death, "maybe I ought not tell y'all. It might hurt y'all's little ears."

"Ah, boy," I said, "don't start that mess again." I didn't like T.J. very much and his stalling around didn't help.

"Come on, T.J.," said Stacey, "out with it."

"Well . . ." T.J. murmured, then grew silent as if considering whether or not he should talk.

We reached the first of two crossroads and turned north; another mile and we would approach the second crossroads and turn east again.

Finally T.J. said, "Okay. See, them Berrys' burnin' wasn't no accident. Some white men took a match to 'em."

"Y-you mean just lit 'em up like a piece of wood?" stammered Christopher-John, his eyes growing big with disbelief.

"But why?" asked Stacey.

T.J. shrugged. "Don't know why. Jus' know they done it, that's all."

"How you know?" I questioned suspiciously.

He smiled smugly. "'Cause your mama come down on her way to school and talked to my mama 'bout it."

"She did?"

"Yeah, and you should've seen the way she look when she come outa that house."

"How'd she look?" inquired Little Man, interested enough to glance up from the road for the first time.

T.J. looked around grimly and whispered, "Like . . . death." He waited a moment for his words to be appropriately shocking, but the effect was spoiled by Little Man, who asked lightly, "What does death look like?"

THE LOGAN FAMILY'S STORY BEGAN IN

THE LAND

★ "Readers . . . will grab this and be astonished by its powerful story."   —*Booklist*, starred review

DAVID LOGAN ENDURES
GROWING TENSIONS IN

THE WELL

"Taylor has used her gift for storytelling and skillful characterization to craft a brief but compelling novel about prejudice and the saving power of human dignity."

—*School Library Journal*

JEREMY SIMMS IMPARTS HIS MEMORY
OF THE LOGANS IN

MISSISSIPPI BRIDGE

"Well written and thought provoking, this book will haunt readers and generate much discussion."

—*School Library Journal*

CASSIE SHARES HER LOVE FOR THE LAND IN

SONG
OF THE
TREES

"A triumphant book . . . A true story truly told."
—*The New York Times Book Review*

THE LOGAN CHILDREN SEE A
LIFELONG BOND TESTED IN

THE
FRIENDSHIP

"A powerful story . . . Readers will be haunted by its drama
and emotion long after they have closed the book."

—*Booklist*

THE LOGAN FAMILY REMAINS UNITED
THROUGH THE LOVE OF FAMILY
AND THEIR LAND IN

ROLL OF THUNDER, HEAR MY CRY

★ "The novel shows the rich inner rewards of black pride, love, and independence." —*Booklist,* starred review

THE LOGAN FAMILY PERSEVERES THROUGH
INCREASINGLY DIFFICULT TIMES IN

LET THE CIRCLE
BE UNBROKEN

"A profoundly affecting novel." —*Publishers Weekly*

As World War II looms, Cassie fights
her own battle in

THE ROAD
to
MEMPHIS

"An engrossing picture of fine young people endeavoring
to find the right way in a world that persistently wrongs
them." —*Kirkus Reviews*